Amelia Bedelia & FRIENDS

Arise and Shine

Daisy

me!

Holly

Joy

Clay

Rose

Skip

Wade

Cliff

Dawn

Heather

Penny
Angel

Amelia Bedelia

& FRIENDS

Arise and Shine

me

by Herman Parish

pictures by Lynne Avril

Greenwillow Books

An Imprint of HarperCollins Publishers

Library of Congress Control Number:2019956756
ISBN 978-0-06-296184-6 (hardback)—ISBN 978-0-06-296183-9 (paperback)
20 21 22 23 24 PC/BRR 10 9 8 7 6 5 4 3 2 1

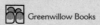 Greenwillow Books

For Shari,

and Nicola—the chivalry expert!

—H. P.

For Genevieve and more adventures!

—L. A.

Amelia Bedelia

Finally

Joy

Clay

Heather

Cliff

Wade

Dawn

Skip

Angel

Penny

Contents

Chapter 1

Medieval Marshmallows

Amelia Bedelia dashed down the stairs and into the kitchen. Her father stood by the stove, spatula in hand. She paused for a moment and inhaled the yummy buttery aroma.

"Blueberry pancakes?" she asked hopefully.

"Blueberry pancakes—

1

aye aye!" he answered, saluting her with his spatula.

Amelia Bedelia wondered why her father had said "Eye eye." She looked at the pancakes with one eye, then the other.

"They look delicious," she said. "And they smell even better. So, nose nose."

Then she remembered why she had run in to the kitchen. "Daddy, do we have any marshmallows?" she asked.

Her father expertly flipped a pancake, then shrugged. "Search me," he said.

"Okay. Empty your pockets, please," said Amelia Bedelia.

Her father put down the spatula and began

2

patting his pockets. "No marshmallows here," he said.

Amelia Bedelia circled her father. She peered up his sleeves and behind his ears. Nothing. She put her hands on her hips. "What about your shoes?" she asked.

"If I had marshmallows in my shoes, I'd be as light as air," Amelia Bedelia's father said with a laugh.

"Don't be silly, Daddy," she said. "You'd be floating around the kitchen if you were as light as air!" She reached for

3

the step stool to look in the cupboard.

Amelia Bedelia climbed up, opened the cupboard door, and started rummaging through the shelves. Among other things, she found a can of sardines (yuck) and four cans of baby corn (yum). But no marshmallows. She sighed, closed the door, and started to climb back down.

Her mother walked into the kitchen, yawning. "What are you looking for, sweetheart?" she asked.

"Marshmallows," said Amelia Bedelia. "For school," she added, in case her mother thought she was making s'mores for breakfast.

s'mores! Her mother thought for a second, then reached into the cabinet above the refrigerator. "Here you go," she said, tossing a bag to her daughter.

Amelia Bedelia caught the marshmallows and hugged them to her chest. "Got them. Thanks, Mom," she said.

Her father put a steaming stack of blueberry pancakes in the middle of the kitchen table, and the family sat down to eat breakfast.

"So why do you need marshmallows?" asked Amelia Bedelia's mother, cutting into her pancakes.

Amelia Bedelia reached for the maple syrup. "We started studying the Middle Ages in school," she said. "Every subject is going to have a special medieval project. Like in science class, we're building catapults. That's what the marshmallows are for. We're making glow-in-the-dark books in Mrs. Shauk's class."

"What books in the Middle Ages glowed in the dark?" asked her father.

Amelia Bedelia was so excited that she kept on talking. "We're even going on a field trip to a medieval fair called the Enchanted Forest!"

"Enchanted Forest!" exclaimed Amelia Bedelia's mother. "I worked there when I was in high school. It was so much fun! I got to wear these long beautiful dresses and had a crown of flowers in my hair. I ran the candle-making stand. I haven't thought about that in years!"

Amelia Bedelia's father stared at her mother, his fork loaded with pancakes halfway to his mouth. "You're pulling my leg," he said. "How did I not know that?"

Amelia Bedelia looked over at her mother. Both of her mother's hands were on the table. "No, she's not, Daddy," she said.

"Not what?" he asked.

"Pulling your leg," said Amelia Bedelia.

"She's right," said Amelia Bedelia's mother. "I'm not pulling your leg at all. I really did work at the fair." She smiled. "I might even find my old costumes in the attic for you. I'd have to take them in before you could wear them."

"Take them in?" Amelia Bedelia wanted to know. "In where?"

"Oh, around the waist, I would guess," said her mother.

Around the Waist? Must be a new store, Amelia Bedelia thought. She had never heard of it before.

8

"The Middle Ages," said her father. "Such a fascinating time."

Amelia Bedelia stared at her parents, then nodded. "Hey! Both of you are in your middle ages, right?"

Her father cleared his throat. "Your mother and I are *middle-aged*. We are not *from* the Middle Ages," he explained.

"Exactly," said Amelia Bedelia's mother.

Middle-Aged

Middle Ages

"Just how old do you think we are, sugar plum?" She looked like she might be a tiny bit insulted.

"Well, Mrs. Shauk says that the Middle Ages were from the years 500 to 1500," said Amelia Bedelia.

$$\begin{array}{r} 2020 \\ -500 \\ \hline 1520 \end{array}$$

$$\begin{array}{r} 2020 \\ -1500 \\ \hline 520 \end{array}$$

"So do the math," said her father. "How old would that make us?"

Amelia Bedelia did some quick subtracting. "That means you two are between five hundred and twenty and one thousand five hundred and twenty years old," she said.

Amelia Bedelia's parents looked at each other, then gave her the same quizzical look.

"Wow. No wonder I feel so tired," said her father. "I need a nap."

"So now how old do you think we are?" asked her mother.

Amelia Bedelia did not want to hurt her parents' feelings. "I think you look really good for your age!" said Amelia Bedelia.

Chapter 2

Sounds like Pheasants

Later that morning, Amelia Bedelia skipped into her classroom.

"Good morning, Amelia Bedelia," Mrs. Shauk sang out from across the room. "You're full of beans today."

Amelia Bedelia was shocked to see her usually very serious

teacher in such a cheerful mood. She didn't tell Mrs. Shauk that she was actually full of pancakes. She was afraid that it might break the happy spell that had come over her.

Chip and Rose were already in the classroom, hard at work. Everyone had a classroom job. Chip and Rose were on Chair Patrol for the month. Every afternoon they stacked the chairs on top of the desks so that Mr. Jack, the custodian, could sweep the floor. And every morning they took the chairs down

and slid them into place under the desks.

CRASH! Chip lost his hold on a chair, and it slipped to the ground.

Amelia Bedelia jumped.

"Butterfingers!" Rose teased him.

Amelia Bedelia shook her head. Chip should have washed his hands after breakfast like she had! He'd have a better grip.

She emptied her backpack as the rest of her friends began to file in. She placed her lunch in the lunch bin and her books, pencil case, and marshmallows inside her desk. Then she went over to the sink and filled

the watering can. Her classroom job was Plant Waterer. It was one of the best jobs, in her opinion. (Much better than Garbage Picker Upper or Cage Cleaner Outer, that was for sure.) Amelia Bedelia also liked Board Eraser, Paper Passer, and Line Leader. In that order.

She walked over to the windows and stuck a finger into the soil in each pot. Yes, the plants were thirsty. She watered them all carefully.

"Why, Amelia Bedelia," Mrs. Shauk called out. "You certainly do have a green thumb!"

Amelia Bedelia sneaked a peek at her thumbs. They were their usual color.

15

After morning announcements, Mrs. Shauk took attendance (Penny was the only one absent) and Dawn delivered it to the office (she was Message Deliverer). Then Mrs. Shauk began the day's lesson.

"The Middle Ages were a very important time in history," she said. "Class, what comes to mind when you think of the Middle Ages?"

"Castles!" said Daisy.

"Kings and queens!" said Teddy.

"Lords!" added Skip.

"Ladies-in-waiting!" Joy chimed in.

"Knights in shining armor!" whispered Angel.

Mrs. Shauk nodded. "You all are correct," she said. "But there is an important group you haven't mentioned."

The class looked at her blankly. They had no clue.

"Give us a hint," said Clay.

"Well, this group made up most of the population during the Middle Ages," Mrs. Shauk explained.

Still no answer. Still lots of blank looks.

Mrs. Shauk tried again. "It sounds like 'presents.'"

"I've got it!" said Cliff. "Pheasants!"

Mrs. Shauk smiled. "You're close,"

she said. "The lords and ladies in medieval times *did* eat many different kinds of birds. But this was a group of people called *peasants*. You see, the lords owned the land and built castles. And the peasants did all the farming and were allowed to live on the land. And they were all protected by the knights."

"So everyone had a job," said

Pheasant   Peasant

Chip. "Just like our class."

"That's right," said Mrs. Shauk. "And today we're going to talk about knights. It took a very long time to become a knight. A boy first started training as a page when he was just seven years old. He helped around the castle and learned all about manners and how to fight. When he was fifteen, he became

a squire. He would serve his knight, help him with his armor, take care of his horse, and fight by his side in battle. And at about the age of twenty-one, if he had proved himself in battle, he would be knighted. Knights had a code of conduct that they pledged to live by. Does anyone know what that code was called?"

"Politeness?" Holly suggested.

"Good manners?" guessed Clay.

"You are close," said Mrs. Shauk. "But there's another word I'm looking for."

"Give us another hint," said Cliff.

"Okay," said Mrs. Shauk. "The word starts with the letter C."

"Courtesy?" said Dawn.

"Close, very close," said Mrs. Shauk.

The classroom was completely quiet as the students tried to come up with the answer.

Then a voice broke the silence, startling everyone.

"Chivalry!"

Amelia Bedelia and her friends swiveled around to see who had spoken.

Chapter 3

Say Good Knight

And there sat Angel, her cheeks bright pink and her hands on her cheeks. She looked just as surprised as everyone else by her outburst.

Mrs. Shauk clapped her red-fingernailed hands together three times. "Bravo, Angel! The code of chivalry was a list of noble qualities that a good knight should possess."

Teddy raised his hand. "Was the code of chivalry a secret code?"

"No," said Mrs. Shauk. "Everyone knew it. Even the peasants."

Clay raised his hand next. "What did the queen say to the knight at the end of the day?"

Then he answered his own question. "Good night, good knight!"

Goodnight, good Knight!

homophones

Everyone just stared at him.

"It's a joke!" he said.

"I don't get it," said Cliff.

"Me neither," said Holly.

Amelia Bedelia was glad she wasn't the only one.

"Very funny, Clay," said Mrs. Shauk with a chuckle. "It's funny because those are two words that sound the same, but are spelled differently and have different meanings," she explained. She wrote both words on the board. "You wish someone a good night, and a knight in shining armor who does kind deeds could be called a good knight. Words like that are called

knight   Good   night

homophones. Can anyone think of another example?"

Amelia Bedelia raised her hand. "You mean like an aunt who's your relative and an ant that's a bug?" she asked.

"Excellent!" said Mrs. Shauk. "Anyone else?"

Holly stood up and flexed her bicep. "I've got one! Like muscles in your arm and mussels from the ocean!"

"Exactly right!" said Mrs. Shauk, writing the new homophones on the board.

"Tell us the joke again, Clay," said Wade.

Clay was more than happy to oblige. "Hey, what did the queen say to the knight at the end of the day?" he asked.

"Good night, good knight!" everyone shouted together. And this time the whole class laughed and laughed. So did Mrs. Shauk. And she didn't even get mad at them for yelling.

"That reminds me," Mrs. Shauk said, once the classroom was quiet again. "There was another job in the castle—the court jester. A jester's job was to entertain everyone in the castle, especially the king."

Clay nodded. "I'd like that job!"

Mrs. Shauk began writing on the board:

court
jester

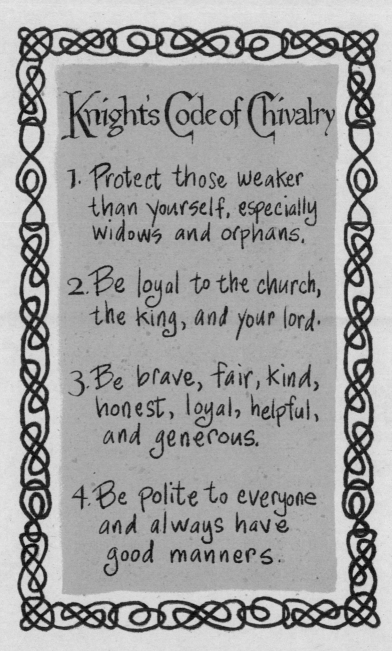

Knight's Code of Chivalry

1. Protect those weaker than yourself, especially widows and orphans.

2. Be loyal to the church, the king, and your lord.

3. Be brave, fair, kind, honest, loyal, helpful, and generous.

4. Be polite to everyone and always have good manners.

Amelia Bedelia stared at the board. Then she had an idea. It wasn't really quite a Big Idea, so she decided to call it a Medium Idea. She raised her hand.

"Mrs. Shauk? We should follow this code in our classroom," she said.

"Interesting suggestion, Amelia Bedelia," said Mrs. Shauk.

"That's a great idea!" said Angel.

"Some of these rules are pretty old-fashioned," said Cliff.

"So why don't we update them?" suggested Mrs. Shauk.

Joy raised her hand. "You mean like instead of 'Protect the weak, especially widows and orphans,' it could say 'Help out a friend who is having trouble'?" she asked.

Mrs. Shauk wrote that down. "That's terrific, Joy," she said. "How about the second rule?"

Wade said, "Let's change it to 'Respect your teachers and principal.'"

"That's good," said Clay. "Just don't forget about Mrs. Roman."

The class murmured in agreement. Mrs. Roman was the assistant to the principal, but everyone (including Mrs. Hotchkiss, the principal) knew that she was the one who kept the school running.

"Or Mr. Jack," said Amelia Bedelia.

"How about 'Respect your teachers and school staff'?" said Dawn.

"Let's add friends too," suggested Chip.

Everyone thought that was a good idea. They also all agreed that rules three and four were fine just the way they were.

"We could call it the code of classroom chivalry!" said Joy.

CLASSROOM CHIVALRY

Mrs. Shauk wrote that in big letters across the top of the board. "You know,

some people say that chivalry is dead,"
she said. She turned to the class. "Let's
prove them wrong!"

Amelia Bedelia liked the idea of
everyone in her class working hard to
be kind and helpful and respectful to one
another. But there was one thing she
didn't get. How could chivalry be dead?
It was never alive in the first place!

Chapter 4

Battering What???

As soon as Amelia Bedelia walked into Ms. Garcia's classroom, she wrinkled her nose. What was that smell? Someone must have left their lunch in the classroom overnight. But she quickly forgot about the odd odor when she spotted the supplies that Ms. Garcia, the science teacher, had piled on their desks. There were dozens of Popsicle sticks, rubber bands, and plastic spoons.

"As we learned earlier," Ms. Garcia said, once everyone was settled, "many people lived in castles in the Middle Ages. Castles were built for safety and protection. They had thick stone walls and high towers and were often surrounded by a ditch filled with water, called a *moat*."

Ms. Garcia leaned forward and lowered her voice as if she was about to tell the class a secret. "The water in the moats sometimes came from the castle toilets," she said.

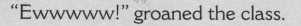
toilet water

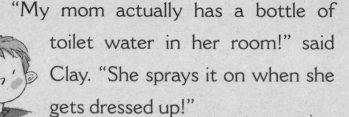

"Ewwwww!" groaned the class.

"My mom actually has a bottle of toilet water in her room!" said Clay. "She sprays it on when she gets dressed up!"

"Gross!" said Cliff.

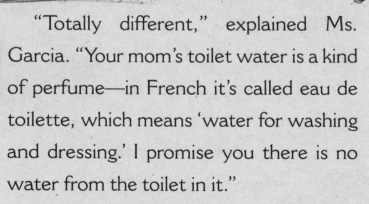

"Totally different," explained Ms. Garcia. "Your mom's toilet water is a kind of perfume—in French it's called eau de toilette, which means 'water for washing and dressing.' I promise you there is no water from the toilet in it."

Clay did not look convinced. "Why did they call it such a disgusting name?"

Pat raised his hand. "So how did people get in and out of the castle if it was surrounded by water?"

"I know!" said Wade. "They just *waded* across!"

"Good one, Wade," said Ms. Garcia. "But they usually got inside another way. Can anyone guess how?"

"They used a draw-bridge," said Angel. "It could be lowered to let people in, then raised to keep enemies out."

Ms. Garcia nodded. "The moat was just one way that castles helped keep people safe from attacks," she said. She showed the students a diagram of

a castle and pointed out each part. "The portcullis was an iron gate that could be pulled down to protect the entrance. The curtain wall was the outer wall. It could be several feet thick. The castle towers let lookouts see enemies approaching from far away. And you'd be safe shooting arrows through the arrow slits in the castle walls. The keep was where everyone ate, slept, and lived. It was in the center of the castle and was the safest place during an attack."

She turned back to the class. "So now that you know how castles are constructed, what kinds of weapons do you think would be the best for storming them?"

"Thunder and lightning?" Amelia Bedelia suggested.

"Not *that* kind of storming," said Ms. Garcia. "More like attacking-the-castle kind of storming."

Amelia Bedelia looked at the diagram of the castle. It was hard to imagine a thick wall made of curtains. Then she looked at the bag of marshmallows she had brought from home,

catapult

and she got an idea. "Oh! Catapults, of course!"

"That's right," said Ms. Garcia. "If soldiers were trying to attack a castle, they would launch heavy stones at the walls to try to knock them down. Sometimes they would shoot flaming tar over the walls to start fires, or even hurl dead animals, like cows. Decaying cows are full of germs, and they could make the people inside sick."

"That's disgusting," said Wade.

"Pretty gross," Ms. Garcia agreed. "They would use siege towers, which were wooden towers on wheels that could

siege tower

be rolled up to the castle. The attackers could climb right over the wall. They also used battering rams to knock down walls and doors."

Amelia Bedelia gasped. She held her head in her hands and said, "Oh no!"

"What's wrong, Amelia Bedelia?" exclaimed Ms. Garcia.

Chapter 5

Ready, Aim, Eat!

The thought of an animal being used to knock down a wall was too much for Amelia Bedelia. "Isn't that cruelty to animals?" she asked. She loved all animals, even the ones that were hard to like, like alligators and warthogs and sharks.

"Don't worry," said Angel. "A battering ram was

usually a long, heavy log that was used to knock down walls and doors," she explained.

"Whew!" said Amelia Bedelia.

Ms. Garcia held up a handmade catapult. "This is a simple machine. It uses a lever (the spoon), with a load, which is the marshmallow, and a fulcrum, which is made out of Popsicle sticks. The force that operates it is your hand."

She placed a marshmallow in the bowl of the spoon and pulled it back. "The spoon is now storing up energy," she explained. Then she aimed the catapult. "When I release the spoon, the energy gets released." She let go, and the marshmallow flew across the room, landing right in the garbage can.

"Once you have built your catapults, test them out and adjust them if you need to. Then we'll head outside to fire at a target. We'll see whose catapult works best. The key to a successful

catapult is accuracy and precision."

"Aren't those the same?" said Pat.

"Not at all. Accuracy is being able to hit the target. Precision is hitting it in the same place every time," said Ms. Garcia. "Accuracy *and* precision would be hitting the same place on the target every time."

"Where do we get flaming tar?" Clay asked with a grin.

"Forget about tar," said Cliff. "We need a herd of dead cows."

Ms. Garcia laughed. "I ran out of both this morning," she joked. "You'll have to settle for marshmallows instead!"

Amelia Bedelia quickly got to work, selecting six Popsicle sticks and fastening them together with rubber bands on each side. Then she picked up two more Popsicle sticks and wrapped an extra-long rubber band around them. She placed the stack of sticks between those two. She looped a rubber band around the entire thing, then attached the spoon to the top Popsicle stick.

"Cliff! Cliff!" Clay called. Amelia Bedelia looked up to see Clay sitting across the table from Cliff, his mouth wide open. Cliff launched the marshmallow, and Clay caught it in his mouth!

That made Amelia Bedelia hungry. She popped a marshmallow into her mouth. Delicious! Then she selected another one and placed it on the spoon.

"Ready . . . aim . . . fire!" she said, pulling back the spoon with her finger. She let go. But her marshmallow didn't fly far at all. *Plop.* It hit the end of the desk and rolled onto the floor. "Awwwww!" said Amelia Bedelia. That was disappointing! Maybe she hadn't pulled the spoon back far enough? She tried again. *Plop.* Same thing.

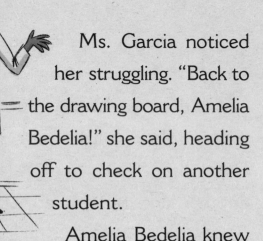

Ms. Garcia noticed her struggling. "Back to the drawing board, Amelia Bedelia!" she said, heading off to check on another student.

Amelia Bedelia knew what that meant. She felt a tap on her shoulder and turned around. It was Angel.

"Can I give you a hand?" asked Angel.

"I've already got two," Amelia Bedelia said. "I just wish I could get my marshmallow to fly."

"I can help you out," said Angel. She studied Amelia Bedelia's catapult. "It looks like you used an extra-long rubber band to lash the two sticks together," she said.

"So you'll have to wrap it around twice as many times so it's tight enough to create tension."

Under Angel's expert eye, Amelia Bedelia tightened the rubber band. Then she aimed and fired. This time her marshmallow soared all the way to the other end of the classroom!

"Thanks, Angel," said Amelia Bedelia. "You sure know a lot about catapults. And the Middle Ages."

"I've been reading lots of books about medieval times," said Angel. "I think it's so cool. Especially the knights and dragons."

Once everyone was

happy with their catapults, they headed outside. The class took turns shooting at the target Ms. Garcia had set up. Some marshmallows fell short. Some sailed right over the target. A few hit it, including Angel's.

Then it was Amelia Bedelia's turn. She remembered everything that Angel had told her. She made sure the rubber bands were still nice and tight. She aimed her catapult, pulled the spoon back, and released it. Her marshmallow went flying across the yard, straight and true. It hit the target dead center.

"Bull's-eye!" said Ms. Garcia. "Great job, Amelia Bedelia."

Amelia Bedelia wasn't sure what a bull or his eye had to do with her catapult, but she was happy just the same. She was even happier when she hit the middle again. Precision *and* accuracy!

"I've got to take my hat off to you guys," said Ms. Garcia when they were through. "You did a great job on your catapults."

Amelia Bedelia stared at her bareheaded teacher. "You already took it off, Ms. Garcia," she said.

"Took off what?" asked Ms. Garcia.

"Your hat," said Amelia Bedelia.

"What hat?" said Ms. Garcia.

"The hat you took off!" said Amelia Bedelia.

Ms. Garcia looked confused. "Was I wearing a hat?" she asked. "Oh, never mind. Who wants marshmallows?"

Naturally, everyone did. Amelia Bedelia and her friends took their seats around their tree-stump table. Ms. Garcia gave them a bag of marshmallows to share.

Angel cleared her throat. "It's like we're the Knights of the Round Table!" she said shyly.

"What are the Knights of the Round Table?" Heather wanted to know.

Ms. Garcia nodded to Angel. "Angel, would you like to tell everyone?"

Her face bright pink, Angel explained. "There was a mythical king named Arthur, who lived in a kingdom called Camelot. He became the king because a magician named Merlin put a sword in a stone. A legend said that whoever was able to pull it out would be the new king. No one was able to pull it out, except for Arthur. The Lady of the Lake gave him a magical

Excalibur

sword called Excalibur. He would meet with his knights around a large round table, so they became known as the Knights of the Round Table. They were the best knights in the kingdom and spent their time fighting for their king and going on quests to right wrongs."

"Nicely done," said Ms. Garcia. "More marshmallows, anyone?"

Amelia Bedelia reached into the bag and took two. She was starting to understand why Angel liked the Middle Ages so much.

Chapter 6

Flying What-Tresses?

Amelia Bedelia's favorite time of day was dinnertime. She and her parents ate together every night and discussed what had happened that day. She liked hearing about what her parents had been up to while she was busy at school.

That night they were having chicken, mashed potatoes, and green beans.

Amelia Bedelia's mom reached over and helped herself to an extra-large helping of potatoes.

"Whoa, Nellie!" said Amelia Bedelia's father. "Leave some for the rest of us!"

"That's Mom, Daddy," said Amelia Bedelia. She served herself next and then passed the spoon to her father.

"So what did you do in school today?" he asked as he poured gravy over his potatoes.

"We played softball in gym today, and I got a hit," she said.

"That's my cupcake," said her mother.

"Then we learned all about cathedrals

54

flying buttress

and flying buttresses," said Amelia Bedelia. "Me and my friends got a big laugh out of that. But they're really very interesting. Did you know that buttresses supported cathedral walls? When they came up with *flying* buttresses, they could make the walls even taller."

"That *is* interesting," said her father.

Amelia Bedelia nodded. "We also studied the Hundred Years' War. Guess how long it lasted."

"Hmmmmm. That's a tough one," said her father, pretending to rack his brain.

"Could it be . . . a hundred years?" he said.

"That's what I figured

too!" exclaimed Amelia Bedelia. "But it actually lasted for one hundred and *sixteen* years!"

"Well, I'll be a monkey's uncle!" said her father.

"Dad!" said Amelia Bedelia. "My cousin, Jason, is not a monkey!"

"Are you sure?" asked Amelia Bedelia's father. He turned to his wife. "You've been very quiet tonight." He took a closer look at her. "What's going on? You look like you're about to burst!"

"She didn't eat *that* many potatoes!" said Amelia Bedelia.

"I do have something to tell you two," her mother said excitedly. "Remember how I thought I might have my old

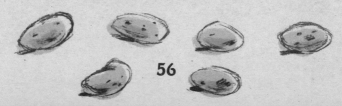

56

medieval costumes somewhere in the attic? Well, I looked and I looked, but I couldn't find them.

"I knew you'd be disappointed, so I called my old employer, the Enchanted Forest, to ask about renting a costume for you. It turns out that the very same people still own it. Sharon and Marty! Can you believe it? They remembered me and offered to lend enough costumes for your whole class to wear when they visit!"

"Oh, wow," said Amelia Bedelia. "I can't wait to tell everyone!"

* * *

Next morning, Mrs. Shauk was thrilled. "Amelia Bedelia, you hit a home run!" she said.

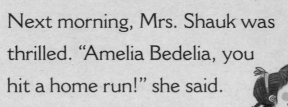

"It was just a single," said Amelia Bedelia.

Mrs. Shauk turned to the rest of the students. "It was very chivalrous of Amelia Bedelia to do such a good deed for the rest of the class," she said. "And Skip, I noticed that you held the door open for Mrs. Roman this morning. That was very polite of you. Has anyone else been practicing classroom chivalry?"

The classroom was silent.

"Um, I said, 'Excuse me,' after I burped

at breakfast," confessed Cliff.

But Mrs. Shauk acted like she did not hear him. And no one else seemed to have any good deeds to share. Mrs. Shauk was disappointed.

"I have an idea!" she said suddenly, clapping her hands. "Why don't we have a competition? The most chivalrous student in class will win a prize. Anything you want. Within reason, of course!"

That got everyone's attention. The ideas started flying.

"No homework for a week?" said Wade.

"Teacher for a day?" said Holly.

"Extra recess?" Cliff said.

"A month off from school?" suggested Clay.

"Yes, yes, yes, and no way," said Mrs. Shauk.

The class got right to work. Pat and Holly were standing in line by the pencil sharpener. Pat stepped aside. "After you, my lady," he told her.

Just then Heather sneezed.

"Bless you, my lady," said Dawn. "May I offer you this box of tissues?"

Mrs. Shauk smiled. "You're going to be the best-behaved class at Oak Tree Elementary!" she said. "Keep up the good work!"

Amelia Bedelia looked around the

room. "Where's Penny?" she asked. "Is she still absent?"

Mrs. Shauk nodded. "She has the flu," she said. "She'll be out another day or two, for sure."

Amelia Bedelia and her friends groaned as they made their way to their seats. Poor Penny!

Mrs. Shauk clapped her hands again. "Today we are going to begin creating our very own illuminated manuscripts," she announced. "Back in medieval times, not everyone was lucky enough to learn to read and write. The nobility usually knew how, and the clergy—priests or monks or high officials of the

church. The printing press had not yet been invented, so books had to be copied by hand, mostly by monks, who used perfect handwriting and then decorated them with beautiful illustrations. One book could take years."

"Years for every book?" said Pat. "They had better be works of art."

"Actually, they are called illuminated manuscripts because the gold and silver leaf that was used on them shines very brightly," Mrs. Shauk explained. "Many medieval manuscripts still glow to this day."

Amelia Bedelia raised her hand. "They might not have been able to read but at least their books glowed in the dark," she said.

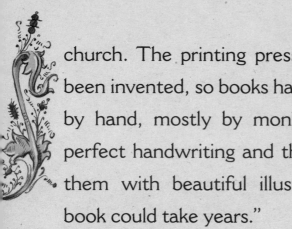

Mrs. Shauk handed out sheets of old-looking parchment paper for the students to use. "I wish I could afford real gold and silver for your manuscripts," she said. "But we'll have to make do with metallic pens."

Amelia Bedelia and her friends eagerly grabbed pens, pencils, paints, and markers.

Amelia Bedelia turned to Skip. "What are you going to write about?"

"Falconry," he said. "Birds of prey are so cool."

Angel raised her hand. "May I please get an extra piece of parchment?"

Mrs. Shauk handed her another sheet.

Amelia Bedelia and her friends chattered excitedly as they discussed the subjects they wanted to tackle. Clay was all about jesters, of course. Heather was thinking about weapons. Angel didn't chat with anyone but went straight to work.

Amelia Bedelia smoothed her hand over the crisp parchment paper. It made a crinkly sound. It was so clean and beautiful, just begging to be written on and drawn on. There was just one problem—she had no idea what in the world she wanted to illuminate.

Chapter 7

A Noble Deed

"PU!" said Skip as he walked into Ms. Garcia's classroom later that day. The smell had gotten so bad that he stopped short in the doorway. Amelia Bedelia bumped right into him.

"Oof!" he said.

"Excuse me, sir," she said.

Skip turned around and

bowed. "Begging your pardon, my lady," he replied. "One whiff of this unsavory air vexes my nostrils!"

Amelia Bedelia stepped into the classroom and sniffed the air. Skip was right. The smell had gotten much worse overnight.

Ms. Garcia walked into the science room. "Gracious! What is that terrible odor?" she said.

Amelia Bedelia was determined to figure out where the smell was coming from. Her nose led her straight to the corner where the two class pets, Harriet the hamster and Hermione the corn snake, lived.

"I think I found it,"

she said. Her voice sounded really weird since she was holding her nose.

"Did you sniff out the problem?" asked Ms. Garcia.

Amelia Bedelia nodded. She certainly had.

"Who is Cage Cleaner Outer this month?" asked Ms. Garcia. The animal cages required weekly cleaning.

Heather looked at the chart. "It's Penny," she said. "And she's still sick!"

CAGE CLEANER-OUTER	
DATE	STUDENT
9/m/x	HOLLY
9/x/x	CLAY
10/x/x	TEDDY
10/x/x	PENNY

"That's unfortunate. Well, luckily we are heading outside today to make sundials," Ms. Garcia said. "But before we go, I'm looking for volunteers to . . ."

A couple of kids raised their hands.

". . . to clean the cages," Ms. Garcia finished.

The hands quickly went back down. Even Daisy, who was usually so helpful, didn't volunteer.

Ms. Garcia sighed. "Looks like I'm going to have to pick someone," she told the class. "We'll see who draws the short straw!"

Amelia Bedelia had no idea who would be drawing straws. Probably the same people who would draw a bridge. Anyway, with her illuminated manuscript project, she had more than enough things to draw at the moment, thank you very much!

The next day Amelia Bedelia and her friends lined up in the hallway in front of Ms. Garcia's room. Ms. Garcia stood in the doorway, a big smile on her face.

"I just wanted to say thank you," she said. "Which one of you wonderful people cleaned the cages for us yesterday?"

Amelia Bedelia stepped inside the room and sniffed the air. Nothing but the usual odor of the tangerine-scented cleaning fluid that Mr. Jack used, plus pencil shavings and maybe a hint of pink eraser. So much better.

But nobody took credit for cleaning the cages.

"I guess our knight in shining armor wishes to remain anonymous," Ms. Garcia said finally. "Well, whoever you are, I am eternally grateful." She nodded. "Okay, time to take out your science notebooks, please. Today we're going to learn about medieval candle clocks."

Amelia Bedelia flipped open her notebook and grabbed her pencil. She wondered who had done the good deed. Talk about chivalry!

Amelia Bedelia was surprised. She noticed that some of her friends were not being chivalrous during Teddy's presentation on medieval beverages. Who knew that beverages were stored in a room called a buttery? And that the beverage keepers were called butlers? And—this was the part that had cracked everyone up—that the beverages were stored in containers called butts?

"When they were empty, did they get recycled into flying buttresses?" asked Clay.

The whole class laughed, except Amelia Bedelia. She really hoped that Mrs. Shauk noticed her polite behavior. She *really* wanted to win the chivalry competition. She was going to ask if they could have show and tell. They hadn't had show and tell since first grade, and she really missed it.

"And who would like to present next?" Mrs. Shauk asked.

Amelia Bedelia sank lower in her seat, hoping not to be picked. She still wasn't done. She looked at the floor, determined not to make eye contact with her teacher. To be truthful, she hadn't even started.

Clay jumped out of his seat. "I'll go!" he said. Then he remembered his manners. "Unless anyone else would like to go first?" When no one spoke up, he placed his parchment on the overhead projector so it could be seen by the entire class. Amelia

Bedelia noticed that the first letter, a W, was illustrated with a jaunty jester's cap. The page was filled with colorful illustrations.

"Why was it so dark in the Middle Ages?" he asked the class. "Because there were so many knights!"

Everyone chuckled. Now they could appreciate a good homophone joke.

"Jesters made a lot of jokes like that one," said Clay. "Their job was to entertain the king and his royal court. Jesters didn't just tell jokes. They also told stories, sang, played instruments, juggled, and danced. But the life of a jester wasn't all fun and games. Sometimes they had to go into battle to deliver secret messages, which was a very dangerous job."

At the end of his presentation, Clay told some more jokes:

"What do you call a knight at the Round Table? Sir Cumference!

"What do you call a knight who always agrees with you? Sir Tenly!

"What do you call a knight who is afraid to fight? Sir Render!

"And last but not least, what do you call a knight who likes to startle people?"

Amelia Bedelia thought for a

second. "Sir Prize?" she guessed.

"Yup!" said Clay.

"Terrific job, Clay," said Mrs. Shauk. "You really engaged your audience. You have set the bar very high for the rest of the class."

Amelia Bedelia gulped. Chivalry, illuminated manuscripts, and now high jumping? Things were getting very complicated!

If Angel wished that Amelia Bedelia would move a little more quickly as they were walking home from school that afternoon, she didn't say a word. Amelia Bedelia was actually dragging her feet. "I still can't decide what to do my illuminated manuscript on," she said with a sigh. "I want it to be something really good!" She turned to Angel. "How much have you done?"

"I'm almost finished," Angel said. "It's all about knights and tournaments, and I used almost an entire silver pen coloring in the armor and . . ." Her voice trailed off when she noticed the look on Amelia Bedelia's face. "I'm sorry, Amelia Bedelia."

"No, I'm glad for you," said Amelia Bedelia. "I just feel bad for me!"

"Well, what do you like most about the Middle Ages?" Angel asked her. "You should write about that."

"Well, I *did* enjoy the story of St. George and the dragon that Mrs. Shauk read today," Amelia Bedelia said.

Angel nodded. "It was a good story," she said.

It was about a brave princess named Sabra who decided to sacrifice herself to a hungry dragon to save the children in her town. How her father wept, and how Sabra fearlessly went to her fate. And how St. George slayed the dragon and saved the day. Amelia Bedelia and her friends thought it was a thrilling story.

"I know you'll figure it out, Amelia Bedelia," said Angel encouragingly. "And you'll do a fantastic job. You always do."

That night after dinner, Amelia Bedelia had a great idea. She would do her illuminated manuscript on mythical medieval creatures! She could just see the illustrations decorating the page—a fire-breathing dragon, a majestic unicorn, a half-lion/half-eagle griffin, a phoenix. She sat down at her desk and started drawing.

But her pictures didn't look anything like she had imagined. To her disappointment,

griffin

her dragon looked like a lumpy lizard, and her unicorn was more like a goat dressed up like a narwhal for Halloween. And don't even ask about her griffin!

Sighing, she slowly erased her sketches. She put on her pajamas and brushed her teeth. She'd think about it in the morning.

Her parents came to her room to tuck her in.

"How is your illuminated manuscript coming along?" asked her mother.

Amelia Bedelia pointed to the blank paper on her desk.

Her mother took a look. "Well, think of it this way. A blank canvas can become anything," she said.

DRAGON

GRIFFIN

UNICORN

"It's a blank parchment," said Amelia Bedelia.

Her mother kissed her on the forehead. "Good night, sweetie," she said.

"Sleep tight," added her father.

"Good night, good knight," Amelia Bedelia replied. It was a private joke, just for herself, but it made her smile.

Chapter 8

A ~~Bad~~ Good Penny Always Turns Up

Amelia Bedelia woke up feeling grumpy. She really wanted to do a good job on her assignment, but time was running out. Even her mother's breakfast of yogurt parfaits, layered with granola and berries, didn't make her smile. She was worried.

"What's wrong, my love, did you wake up on the wrong side of the bed?" asked

81

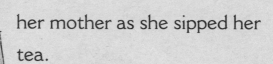

her mother as she sipped her tea.

"Oh, Mom, you know my bed is against the wall," said Amelia Bedelia. "There's only one side to get out of."

But Amelia Bedelia's mood improved considerably when she walked into school and spotted Penny down the hallway. She hurried to catch up with her friend.

"Penny, you're back!" shouted Amelia Bedelia. She gave her a big hug. "Are you feeling okay?"

"I'm much better now," said Penny. "But I was as sick as a dog."

"Gross," said Amelia Bedelia.

Gross

She hated it when Finally got sick.

Mrs. Shauk was delighted to see Penny, as well. "Welcome back, my dear!" she said. She quickly filled her in on what she had missed, while everyone else got settled. "And today the students who are ready will be presenting their illuminated manuscripts," she finished.

Well, at least I'm not the only one who still hasn't finished, thought Amelia Bedelia.

But to her surprise, Penny reached into her backpack and pulled out a neatly rolled sheet of parchment. "I'm ready!" she said.

"My goodness!" said Mrs. Shauk. "How is that possible?"

"A friend dropped

83

off my assignments for me," Penny informed her.

"How lovely," said Mrs. Shauk. "And who was this thoughtful person?"

Penny shook her head. "I promised not to tell," she said.

"The sign of true chivalry," said Mrs. Shauk. "Doing a good deed without expecting a reward." She pointed to the projector. "Go ahead, Penny. You're up."

Penny stood and walked to the front of the room. "My illuminated manuscript is called 'The Black Death.' I chose this subject because I was sick and also because I want to be a doctor someday," she said.

"The Black Death was the name

given to a terrifying outbreak of a disease called the bubonic plague," she told everyone. "It was spread by fleas on rats, which were brought to Europe on trading ships."

rats

The class leaned forward to listen. They didn't want to miss a word. They weren't disappointed. Penny's presentation was fascinating, scary, and gross. Penny adjusted her parchment on the projector.

"Ewwwww," said the class. Some of Penny's illustrations looked extremely realistic!

"After a person was bitten by a flea, the infection would

85

 *flea*

spread to their lymph nodes, which are found on your neck, armpits, and groin. The nodes would swell and turn black," she said. "It was an incredibly contagious disease. Scientists think that it wiped out fifty to sixty percent of the population of Europe."

"What an informative presentation, Penny," said Mrs. Shauk, rubbing her neck absentmindedly. "Very interesting and full of details!" She turned to the class. "I'm on the edge of my seat waiting to see what the rest of you have in store for us."

That's odd, thought Amelia Bedelia. Because Mrs. Shauk wasn't sitting on a seat at all. She was standing up!

86

Chapter 9

Saved by the Knock

On Monday, the presentations continued. Skip presented falconry. Holly taught everyone about the Magna Carta. Amelia Bedelia thought that learning about hunting with birds of prey was much more interesting than learning about a historical document, but she very chivalrously gave both of them her undivided attention. As student after student presented, Amelia Bedelia grew more nervous. It was getting closer and closer to her turn. She dreaded telling Mrs. Shauk she hadn't even started yet.

Finally her time was up. It was the day before they were going to the fair. Mrs. Shauk looked at her list and said, "I think we have just one more presentation to go." She turned to Amelia Bedelia. "You're next, Amelia Be—"

Just then there was a sharp rap on the classroom door.

Joy leaned across the aisle. "Saved by the bell," she said.

"I think you mean saved by the knock,"

Amelia Bedelia said with a sigh of relief.

Mrs. Shauk opened the door and said, "Hello! You must be the owners of the Enchanted Forest!"

An older man and woman stood there smiling. They each held several garment bags.

"Hello!" said the woman cheerfully. "My name is Sharon, and this is my husband, Marty. We heard that your class is visiting our medieval fair tomorrow and we wanted to make sure you would all be properly dressed!"

The class watched with excitement as Sharon and Marty began unzipping

Medieval Clothing

Men

breeches

shirts

gipon

tights

jerkin

turban

cape

Women

wimple

cloak

girdle belt

long dresses

horned headdress

stockings

Medieval Costumes

knight's helmet and breastplate

wizard's costume

monk's robe

jester's costume

the bags and pulling out colorful medieval clothing—breeches, stockings, shirts, gipons, jackets, and cloaks. Long dresses, girdles, wimples, capes, turbans, hats, and headdresses. There was also a jester's costume, a knight's helmet and breastplate, a monk's robe, and even a wizard costume with a high pointed hat. Everyone got something special to wear.

Cliff got the jester's costume but immediately handed it to Clay.

Clay put on the colorful jester's cap. "May I?" he asked Mrs. Shauk, pointing to the bowl of apples on her desk. She nodded and he started juggling them, to everyone's delight.

Sharon stopped in front of

Amelia Bedelia's desk. "Amelia Bedelia?" she asked. "I saved a special costume just for you."

She handed Amelia Bedelia a purple dress with golden embroidery on the bodice.

Marty plunked a crown on her head. "Princess Amelia Bedelia," he said.

Amelia Bedelia clutched the dress to her chest. It was beautiful.

Pat walked over to Amelia Bedelia's desk, holding a knight's breastplate in one hand and a helmet in the other. "Look at my costume!" he said. "It's amazing!"

Angel turned around, holding a pink dress and wearing a wreath of flowers on her head. "I really like your costume," she said.

"Thank you," said Amelia Bedelia and Pat at the same time. They laughed.

"I like yours too," said Amelia Bedelia.

"Sharon said I'm a lady-in-waiting," said Angel. "Maybe I'm *your* lady-in-waiting," she said. Then she sighed.

"Would you rather be a princess?" asked Amelia Bedelia. She offered Angel the purple dress. "I'll trade with you and be your lady-in-waiting."

Angel shook her head. "That's really kind, Amelia Bedelia. But no, thank you," she said.

Soon all the costumes had been handed out. "See you tomorrow," called Sharon.

"We're looking forward to seeing you at the fair," said Marty. "I know you'll all have a royally good time!"

"Don't forget to wear your costumes to school tomorrow!" Mrs. Shauk reminded the students as they packed up at the end of the day. When Amelia Bedelia walked past, Mrs. Shauk stopped her. "I'm sorry you didn't get a chance to present today," she said. "Since we'll be out tomorrow, you can present the day after tomorrow. I can't wait to find out what your illuminated manuscript is all about."

Amelia Bedelia gulped. She couldn't wait to find out either!

Chapter 10

Your School Bus Awaits

The next morning, Amelia Bedelia and Pat reached the classroom at the same time.

Pat bowed, his armor clanking. "After you, Your Highness," he said.

Amelia Bedelia curtsied. As she

did, the crown fell off her head and rolled
down the hallway. She chased after it, put
it back on, and went into the classroom.
Mrs. Shauk's normally peaceful room was
now a scene from the Middle Ages. It
was crowded with peasants, lords, ladies,
a knight, a monk, and a jester.

"You look great, Amelia Bedelia!"
Penny called out.

"You do too," said Amelia Bedelia.

Penny was dressed as a noble lady in a

pretty blue dress. "I like your headdress," said Amelia Bedelia.

Mrs. Shauk and Ms. Garcia stood at the front of the room, counting permission slips. They both wore long dresses with belts. Their hair was tucked under white caps.

Mrs. Shauk checked her watch. "It's almost time!" she said. "Let's head outside."

The class was buzzing as they marched down the hallway. Mrs. Roman poked her head out of the office as they passed. At first it looked like she was about to scold them for making noise in the hallway. But then she smiled. "You all look great!" she called out. "Have fun in the fifteenth century!"

As they headed toward the bus, Clay

scooped up an acorn and tried balancing it on his nose. He walked right into Pat, who was clearly having trouble seeing through his knight's visor.

"Pardon me!" they both said at the exact same time.

"Here comes our time machine!" Ms. Garcia said.

Time machine? All Amelia Bedelia saw was their regular old yellow school bus pulling up to the curb.

"Let's imagine it's a cart or a carriage," said Joy. "That's what they used for transportation in the Middle Ages."

Amelia Bedelia gathered her long skirts and climbed aboard.

WELCOME TO THE ENCHANTED FOREST read the sign on the front gate when they arrived. The gate was covered in garlands of ivy and brightly colored flowers. Sharon and Marty themselves were waiting to greet the bus. They were dressed as a king and queen, complete with fake-fur-trimmed robes and lots of fancy jewelry.

"We're so pleased you are here at the Enchanted Forest!" Sharon said. "In the Middle Ages, people worked very hard, from sunup till sundown. There wasn't much time for relaxing or having fun. So the fairs, which happened several times a year, were very important. It was a time to stop working and to eat, drink, listen to music, and dance with your neighbors."

She turned to Marty, who continued, "We have a full day of activities for you so you can really enjoy the medieval experience. You'll see a live falconry demonstration, design your very own coat of arms, have a medieval feast for lunch, learn how to make candles, and root for your favorite knight at a joust

before the day is through. You might even see a dancing bear, if you're lucky!"

"Have a wonderful time, everyone!" Sharon concluded.

Angel was so excited she squeezed Amelia Bedelia's arm a little too tightly.

Ouch!

"Ouch," said Amelia Bedelia.

"Begging your pardon," Angel said.

"No problem!" said Amelia Bedelia. She understood. She was almost as excited as Angel was.

Mrs. Shauk led the way through the gate. The dirt path was lined with thatched cottages and open-air stalls. Amelia Bedelia could see a blacksmith working

blacksmith

baker

the bellows as he tended a
fire. Nearby, a baker shaped
dough into loaves. A woman was deep
in concentration as she wove flowers
into a colorful floral crown. Townspeople
strolled through the streets in costume,
baskets over their arms as
they did their marketing.
Someone was even walking
a goat on a rope!

At the end of the path, a crowd had
gathered. Amelia Bedelia and her friends
joined in. They found a jester telling jokes
as he juggled colorful balls in the air.

The jester spotted Clay in his costume.
"Ah, a fellow jester!" he said. "My name is
Jester John. Care to join me?" He tossed

the balls to Clay.

Clay was taken by surprise. He caught the first ball but fumbled the others. Flustered, he picked them up and started to juggle. But then he dropped the balls again.

"Sorry," Clay muttered as he handed them back to Jester John.

Poor Clay, thought Amelia Bedelia. That was so unlike him. He was usually so good at entertaining a crowd.

Clay unhappily dragged his jingle-belled, curly-toed feet as they made their way to their first stop, the falconry show. They walked through some trees into a clearing, the grassy center

falcon

surrounded by rows of wooden benches. A man wearing a leather vest and a thick leather glove that went all the way up his arm stood next to a dark brown bird with reddish tail feathers sitting on a perch.

Amelia Bedelia and her friends took their seats. Pat was on one side of Amelia Bedelia, and Angel was on the other. Skip, who had done his illuminated manuscript on falconry, sat right in front. He wore the long brown robe of a medieval monk, with a rope belt and a heavy hood.

"My name is Andrew, and I am a master falconer," said the man. "Falconry is the art of hunting with birds of prey.

hawk

Birds that are used in falconry are hawks, falcons, and sometimes owls. This is Sir William, a red-tailed hawk."

Amelia Bedelia and her friends tried not to giggle. Mrs. Shauk was also known as the Hawk, because she saw everything, even with her back turned.

Andrew continued, "Birds of prey have sharp talons, hooked beaks, and excellent eyesight. They can see eight times better than a human. Falconry is thought to have originated in China and been introduced to Europe by the explorer Marco Polo. At first people used the birds to help them hunt for their dinners. But then it became

Marco Polo

quite popular among the nobility, and remained so for four hundred years. Almost everyone had their very own bird of prey, and people would walk down the streets with their birds on their arms."

Andrew the Falconer held up his arm. "Does anyone know what this glove is called?"

"A gauntlet," said Skip. "It protects your arm from the bird's talons."

gauntlet

"Very good!" said Andrew. "And do you know why Sir William has bells on his legs?"

"So you can find him if he doesn't come back right away," Skip answered confidently.

"Someone has done their homework!" said Andrew.

How in the world did he know that Skip did his report on falconry? Amelia Bedelia wondered.

Andrew then gave Sir William a command and pointed behind them, to another perch. Sir William took off and silently soared over everyone's heads. Andrew called him, and Sir William flew back overhead. Amelia Bedelia looked up and noticed that Sir William was almost all white underneath, with dark wing tips.

Amelia Bedelia glanced over at Pat. His eyes were tightly closed.

"What's wrong, Pat?" she asked.

Pat opened his eyes. "I was afraid Sir William was going to poop on my armor!" he said.

"He missed," Amelia Bedelia told him with a laugh.

Andrew pointed to Skip. "How would you like to come up and have Sir William land on your arm?" he asked.

Skip stood up. But when Sir William opened his mouth and gave a loud, hoarse screech, Skip sat right back down. "Um, maybe I'll let someone else have a chance," he said sheepishly.

Andrew addressed the class. "Would anyone else like to volunteer?"

Without a moment's hesitation, Angel walked

up to Andrew and Sir William. Andrew put the huge gauntlet over her small fist, and she held out her arm.

Sir William circled overhead several times, then came in for a landing. Amelia Bedelia winced when she saw his sharp talons flashing. But Angel didn't even blink. To Amelia Bedelia's surprise (and disgust), Angel even fed the bird some raw meat!

It was time to go create their own coats of arms. Amelia Bedelia hurried to catch up to Angel. "Wow, you were so brave," Amelia Bedelia told her.

Angel smiled. "It was great!" she

said. "I love anything that has to do with animals. I don't even mind feeding my snake or cleaning his cage."

"I love animals too," said Amelia Bedelia. "Did you know that we got my dog, Finally, from—" All of a sudden Amelia Bedelia was almost knocked over. An animal dashed past, trailing a rope.

"Stop that goat!" a man called, racing after it.

He didn't need to ask twice. Amelia Bedelia and her friends took off.

Chapter 11

A Second Chance

The chase was on! Amelia Bedelia and her friends followed the runaway goat over the wishing bridge, past the archery exhibit, and around the maypole. Twice. The goat bounded through the fairy garden, leaped over a giant toadstool, and somehow got a string of colorful pennants tangled

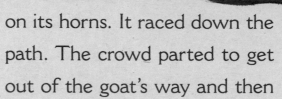

on its horns. It raced down the path. The crowd parted to get out of the goat's way and then stood and watched as Amelia Bedelia and her friends raced by. It was like they were watching the world's shortest—and fastest—parade.

Amelia Bedelia surged ahead of the group and was hot on the goat's heels, her crown clutched in one hand and her skirt gathered in the other. Just then the goat took a sharp left into one of the stalls and didn't come back out. Amelia Bedelia stepped inside quietly. There was the goat, nosing around at a table.

"*Baaaaaa*," said Amelia Bedelia. She wasn't sure if that was what goats said.

Maybe it was just sheep. But to her surprise, it worked, because the goat turned around.

Amelia Bedelia let out a laugh. The goat was lazily chewing on a fat brown candle, looking just like an old man chomping on a cigar. Amelia Bedelia grabbed the rope and led the goat outside.

"I got your goat!" she told the man who had been chasing it.

The man laughed. "Good one! You certainly did! But in this case, you made me happy, not annoyed."

Amelia Bedelia nodded. Of course! Who wouldn't be

happy to have a goat? She was feeling pretty proud of herself as she and her friends headed to a nearby tent to learn about coats of arms.

A knight named Sir Charles introduced himself, holding up a shield with a red dragon on a blue background. "Knights started decorating their shields so they could be identified in battle. Everyone was in armor, so it was hard to tell friend from foe. In time, coats of arms became popular among regular people too. Sometimes people chose a symbol that represented their occupation or their name. Others picked a design just because they liked it.

A herald kept a book with a record of all the motifs to make sure that no two coats of arms were the same."

Sir Charles then led them to the paint tables, where cardboard shield shapes were laid out. When the silver background she had painted had dried, Amelia Bedelia decided to paint one of her favorite things. It was hard to decide. Should she paint Finally? A stack of blueberry pancakes? Her parents? A lemon tart? She couldn't choose. Then she decided— she'd paint all of them!

When she was done, she smiled. It was royally perfect and would be a great souvenir to take home and hang on her bedroom wall.

Grrrrrrrrrrrr!

"Was that the dancing bear?" asked Pat.

"No, that's just Clay's stomach growling," said Heather.

"Um, excuse me," Clay said. "But I'm hungry enough to eat a horse!" Luckily, it was time for their medieval lunchtime feast. Amelia Bedelia just hoped that horse was not on the menu!

Amelia Bedelia and her friends sat down at long tables under a tent. The medieval waiters and waitresses placed pieces of bread in front of them.

"I think they forgot our plates," Holly whispered. She tapped the bread, which was as hard as a rock. "And this bread is stale!"

"These are trenchers," explained Angel. "There were no plates in medieval times, so people used stale bread to eat from, like this."

"There were also no forks," explained the head waitress, whose name tag read *Patricia*. "So you'll notice that you only have knives and spoons! And people ate with their hands too."

Wade asked the question everyone

119

was thinking. "Isn't that bad manners?"

Patricia laughed. "Not in medieval times, it wasn't!"

It was weird at first, but then everyone started getting into the experience. Even Mrs. Shauk seemed to enjoy eating with her hands! Amelia Bedelia picked up a turkey leg and chomped away. The droopy extra-long sleeves of her costume kept dragging on her trencher, so she rolled them up.

"No plates or forks makes it easier to do the dishes," said Amelia Bedelia.

"This is a simple feast," said the head waitress, as she handed out piping-hot meat pies. "But sometimes, for a special occasion, a feast in a castle could be quite elaborate. There could be hundreds of guests. People ate wild game like deer, boar, pigeons, and cranes.

Sometimes peacocks and swans were cooked, and then the feathers were put back on the birds before they were served. Very fancy feasts might serve things we consider quite odd today, such as seals, porpoises, and whales."

"I'll stick with turkey!" said Ms. Garcia. She had a drumstick in one hand and a potato in the other. "And these potatoes!"

"Have you heard of the nursery rhyme 'Sing a song of sixpence, a pocket full of rye, four and twenty blackbirds baked in a pie'?" Patricia asked. "Cooks would put live birds under a pie crust after it had been baked. When the pie was cut open at a feast, the birds flew out."

Mrs. Shauk laughed. "That's strictly for the birds!" she said.

After lunch they headed over to the tournament field. The class was divided into two groups as they filed into the stands. Amelia Bedelia's group was given small red flags so they could root for the red knight, and the other group was given blue flags so they could root for the blue knight. The stands faced a large fenced-in area with a long white rail running down the middle.

While they waited for the joust to begin, Jester John appeared and began telling jokes. But he had barely gotten started before a page ran over.

"King Marty needs you right away!" the page cried.

To everyone's surprise, Jester John reached into the stands and pulled Clay out by the hand. "Keep everyone amused, will you?" he asked before he ran off.

Clay stood in front of the crowd. "Um . . . hi," he managed to squeak

out. Then he giggled nervously.

"This is terrible!" said Cliff. "Someone needs to do something!"

Just then Angel leaned toward Amelia Bedelia. "Knock knock," she whispered in Amelia Bedelia's ear.

"Knock what?" said Amelia Bedelia, confused. Her eyes were on Clay.

"It's a joke for Clay," Angel whispered. "Yell 'Knock knock.'"

"Knock knock!" Amelia Bedelia called out.

Clay looked at her like she was crazy. "Um, who's there?" he said finally.

"Joust," Angel whispered.

"Joust!" called Amelia Bedelia.

"J-joust who?" said Clay.

Angel whispered in Amelia Bedelia's ear.

"Joust wanted to tell you it's time to tell some jokes!" shouted Amelia Bedelia.

The crowd laughed and applauded. And suddenly Clay was Clay again. He told all of his jester jokes— and then some. Jester John returned, and the two ended up juggling together. And this time Clay didn't drop a thing. The two jesters got a standing ovation.

Mrs. Shauk turned around in her seat and gave Amelia Bedelia a thumbs-up. "Good job!" she said. "You broke the ice!"

Amelia Bedelia was pretty sure they didn't have freezers in the Middle Ages, but maybe they got ice from frozen rivers? That would make sense. But before Amelia Bedelia could figure out what Mrs. Shauk was talking about, the show began. Amelia Bedelia settled into her seat, clutching her flag.

The blare of a trumpet and the beating of a drum signalled that the tournament was about to begin.

"Welcome to the Enchanted Forest tournament!" an announcer boomed. "Introducing the blue knight and the red knight!"

The two knights appeared, mounted on horses who pranced around the field. The knights were dressed from head to toe in shiny armor, and their horses wore fancy embroidered coats in their knight's colors. The knights waved to the crowd, and the crowd cheered. The knights both held long lances and each had a shield attached to his armor.

"And now the knights will take their positions!" said the announcer. "The knights will have three chances to hit, break, or knock off their opponent's shield. A hit earns one point, a break earns two, and knocking it off completely earns three.

The knight with the most points will win!"

The drum beat faster and faster as the knights took their places on either side of the rail. Amelia Bedelia waved her flag as they charged, their

lances aimed at each other.

Crash! Both knights had made contact. The score was one to one.

On the second round, the blue knight broke off a piece of the red knight's shield. The red knight made contact, but the blue knight's shield was still whole. That meant the score was now three to two. The blue knight was winning. Amelia Bedelia was worried.

"This final round will determine the winner!" called the announcer. Amelia Bedelia held her breath as the two knights thundered toward each other. *CRASH!* Pieces of wood went flying. But who was the winner? Amelia Bedelia leaned forward to see their shields.

The announcer cleared things up. "The blue knight has made a hit, but the red knight has destroyed the blue knight's shield. The red knight is the winner!"

The crowd clapped and cheered as the red knight took a victory lap around the field. Then both knights got off their horses. The blue knight took off his helmet and threw it to the ground. *Sore loser!* thought Amelia Bedelia. Then she watched as the red knight took off his helmet and shook out his long, blond . . .

Angel gasped. Amelia Bedelia took a closer look and corrected herself. The red knight was shaking out *her* long, blond hair. Then she took a deep bow to the cheers of the crowd.

Afterward, Amelia Bedelia and her friends

mobbed both knights, asking questions and petting the horses. Angel ran over

to talk to the red knight. The red knight handed Angel her lance, and though Angel had to grip it with both her hands, she hoisted it high in the air.

Look at Angel's face! Amelia Bedelia said to herself. *She's so happy!* Angel obviously loved the Middle Ages.

✳ ✳ ✳

Soon it was time to go. Amelia Bedelia sat down on the school bus and yawned.

Penny climbed on board and plopped down next to Amelia Bedelia. "That was really nice when you helped Clay with that joke," Penny told her.

"Oh, that was actually Angel," explained Amelia Bedelia. "She whispered it to me. I just said it out loud."

"I should have known," said Penny. "Angel is so helpful. She's the one who . . ." Her voice trailed off.

"The one who what?" asked Amelia Bedelia.

"I'm not supposed to tell," said Penny.

Amelia Bedelia's eyes widened. "Angel was the one who brought you your homework, wasn't she?" She had a sudden realization. "And I bet she's the one who cleaned the cages too!"

Penny nodded. "You're probably right," she said.

"She's like a knight in shining armor," said Amelia Bedelia. Then everything made perfect sense. Angel's interest in the Middle Ages. How much she loved the joust. The coat of arms she had made. Her illuminated manuscript. Angel hadn't been wishing for Amelia Bedelia's costume, she had been envying Pat's.

Amelia Bedelia had just realized two
very important things.

Angel wanted to be a knight.

And Amelia Bedelia finally knew what
she was going to do for her illuminated
manuscript.

Chapter 12

Arise and Shine!

Once upon a time there was a young girl named Angel. She was kind and smart and considerate. She was also very nice to animals of all types. She never called attention to herself.

Most of her good deeds (and there were many) were

performed in private.

Angel lived her life by the code of chivalry, helping

Helpful!!

Generous!

those who needed her assistance.

Loyal!

Sometimes Angel did good deeds that no one else wanted to tackle.

Kind!

Or stepped forward to help out in a moment of need.

Angel was always fair and polite, and she had wonderful manners.

BraVE!

Angel didn't do good deeds for praise or attention. She believed in doing the right thing. She didn't expect anything in return. That was not her way.

But good deeds should be rewarded. And although she would never mention it, there was one thing that Angel wanted more than anything else in the world. It was a secret deep in her heart.

Amelia Bedelia stopped reading her illuminated manuscript and looked at Mrs. Shauk.

"I nominate Angel to win the most chivalrous student award," Amelia Bedelia said. "And I think that she should be knighted as her prize."

"Indeed!" said Mrs. Shauk. She turned to Angel. "Is that true, Angel? Would you like to be knighted?"

"More than anything," said Angel. Then she smiled. "And maybe we could have a class pizza party also?"

"Sounds delicious, and it will bring us all back to our century," said Mrs. Shauk.  "Thank you for all the wonderful things you have done around the classroom, Angel. You truly are inspiring. Even the prize you've chosen benefits the whole class!" Then she turned to Amelia Bedelia. "You finally finished your illuminated manuscript, *and* you helped a deserving classmate. Talk about killing two birds with one stone!"

Amelia Bedelia looked horrified. "I would never do that!" she exclaimed. But then she smiled. "But I *did* get two things done at the same time!"

She looked up at her illuminated manuscript, projected on the classroom wall. It didn't matter that her dragon still resembled a lumpy lizard and that Angel's armor looked a bit dented. The expression on the real Angel's face (a little bit embarrassed and a whole lot pleased) made Amelia Bedelia feel like her drawings were a work of art.

At recess, Angel put on the suit of armor and knelt at Amelia Bedelia's feet. Amelia Bedelia took a deep breath and straightened her crown, which had slipped over one eye. She picked up a yardstick and tapped Angel on the left shoulder.

"In honor of your good service, kind nature, generosity, bravery in the face of stinkiness, and all-around helpfulness . . ." She tapped Angel on the right shoulder. "I dub thee Sir Angel, honorary knight of the Oak Tree Elementary Round Table!" Amelia Bedelia pronounced, tapping Angel on the head.

Everyone cheered.

Angel looked up at Amelia Bedelia, a happy smile on her face. "Thank you," she said simply.

"Arise and shine, good knight," said Amelia Bedelia. "The thanks all go to *you* for being our class angel every day."

Afterward, Clay came up to Amelia Bedelia. "I'm confused," he said. "I thought Angel was a lady-in-waiting."

Amelia Bedelia grinned. "She was. A lady-in-waiting . . . to be a knight!"

Mrs. Shauk smiled. "You can say that again!"

"Okay, I will," said Amelia Bedelia. "She was. A lady-in-waiting . . . to be a knight!"

Two Ways to Say It
By Amelia Bedelia

"You have a green thumb."

"You are good at growing plants."

"Search me."

"I don't know."

"I've got to take my hat off to you."

"You were very impressive."

"You're pulling my leg."

"You're kidding me."

"You look like you're about to burst."

"You look like you want to say something."

"Draw the short straw."

"Get the worst choice."

"You broke
the ice."

"You got
people talking."

"I'm on the edge
of my seat."

"I'm very excited."

"I got your goat."

"I annoyed you."

"Kill two birds
with one stone."

"Get two things done
at the same time."

❤ The Amelia Bedelia Chapter Books

With Amelia Bedelia, anything can happen!

Amelia Bedelia **Means Business**

by Herman Parish pictures by Lynne Avril

Amelia Bedelia **Unleashed**

by Herman Parish pictures by Lynne Avril

Amelia Bedelia **Road Trip!**

by Herman Parish pictures by Lynne Avril

Amelia Bedelia **Goes Wild!**

by Herman Parish pictures by Lynne Avril

Amelia Bedelia **Shapes Up**

by Herman Parish pictures by Lynne Avril

Amelia Bedelia **Cleans Up**

by Herman Parish pictures by Lynne Avril

Have you read them all?

Amelia Bedelia Sets Sail
by Herman Parish pictures by Lynne Avril

Amelia Bedelia Dances Off
by Herman Parish pictures by Lynne Avril

Amelia Bedelia On the Job
by Herman Parish pictures by Lynne Avril

Amelia Bedelia Ties the Knot
by Herman Parish pictures by Lynne Avril

Amelia Bedelia Makes a Splash
by Herman Parish pictures by Lynne Avril

Amelia Bedelia Digs In
by Herman Parish pictures by Lynne Avril

Introducing...
Amelia Bedelia
& FRIENDS

Amelia Bedelia +
Good Friends =
Super Fun Stories
to Read and Share

Amelia Bedelia and her friends celebrate their school's birthday.

Amelia Bedelia and her friends discover a stray kitten on the playground!

Amelia Bedelia and her friends take a school trip to the Middle Ages that is as different as knight and day.

Coming

soon . . .

HOW TO BUILD A CATAPULT

Materials: 10 popsicle sticks
5 rubber bands
Plastic spoon (soup spoon preferred)
Marshmallows

Directions:

1. Stack 8 popsicle sticks and wrap both ends tightly with a rubber band.

2. Stack two popsicle sticks and wrap one end tightly with a rubber band.

3. Take the two sticks and pull open the non-wrapped end. Place the stack of eight popsicle sticks between the two sticks. Push the stack of eight popsicle sticks as far as you can to the wrapped end.

4. Wrap a rubber band around the middle where both stacks meet.

5. Place the plastic spoon on the top stick. The bowl of the spoon should be facing up and should extend past the stick. Push the handle of the spoon under the rubber band of the top popsicle stick.

6. Wrap another rubber band around the spoon, just under the bowl.

7. Place a marshmallow in the bowl of the spoon. Secure the front end of the catapult with one hand and pull back the spoon with the other. Let go of the spoon and let the marshmallow fly!

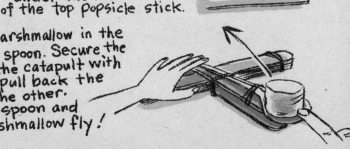